What happens when the hunter becomes the hunted?

To the Gregg family, hunting is just plain fun. To the girl who lives next door, it's just plain horrible. She tries to be polite. She tries to talk them out of it, but the Greggs only laugh at her. Then one day the Greggs go too far, and the little girl turns her Magic Finger on them. When she's very, very angry, the little girl's Magic Finger takes over. She really can't control it, and now it's turned the Greggs into birds! Before they know it, the Greggs are living in a nest, and that's just the beginning of their problems . . .

Puffin Books by Roald Dahl

The BFG

Boy: Tales of Childhood

Charlie and the Chocolate Factory

Charlie and the Great Glass Elevator

Danny the Champion of the World

Dirty Beasts

The Enormous Crocodile

Esio Trot

Fantastic Mr. Fox

George's Marvelous Medicine

The Giraffe and the Pelly and Me

Going Solo

James and the Giant Peach

The Magic Finger

Matilda

The Minpins

The Missing Golden Ticket and Other Splendiferous Secrets

Revolting Rhymes

The Twits

The Vicar of Nibbleswicke

The Witches

The Wonderful Story of Henry Sugar and Six More

ROALD DAHL

THE MAGIC FINGER

Illustrated by
Quentin Blake

PUFFIN BOOKS

This book is for Ophelia and Lucy

PUFFIN BOOKS
An imprint of Penguin Random House LLC
375 Hudson Street
New York, New York 10014

First published in the United States of America by Harper & Row, Publishers, 1966
First published in Great Britain by Allen & Unwin, 1968
Published with illustrations by Quentin Blake in Great Britain by Penguin Books Ltd., 1995
Published in the United States of America by Viking, a division of Penguin Books USA Inc., 1996
Published by Puffin Books (U.S.A.), 1997
Reissued by Puffin Books, 1998
This edition reissued by Puffin Books, an imprint of
Penguin Young Readers Group, 2009, 2013

THE LIBRARY OF CONGRESS HAS CATALOGED THE PREVIOUS PUFFIN BOOKS EDITION AS FOLLOWS:
Dahl, Roald
The magic finger / Roald Dahl;
illustrated by Quentin Blake.
p. cm.
Summary: Angered by a neighboring family's sport hunting,
an eight-year-old girl turns her magic finger on them.
ISBN 978-0-14-038616-5 (pbk)
[1. Hunting—Fiction. 2. Magic—Fiction.] I. Blake, Quentin, ill.—II. Title.
PZ7.D1212Mag—1997 [Fic]—dc21 96-45417 CIP AC

This edition ISBN 978-0-14-241385-2

Printed in the United States of America

27 29 28 26

THE MAGIC FINGER

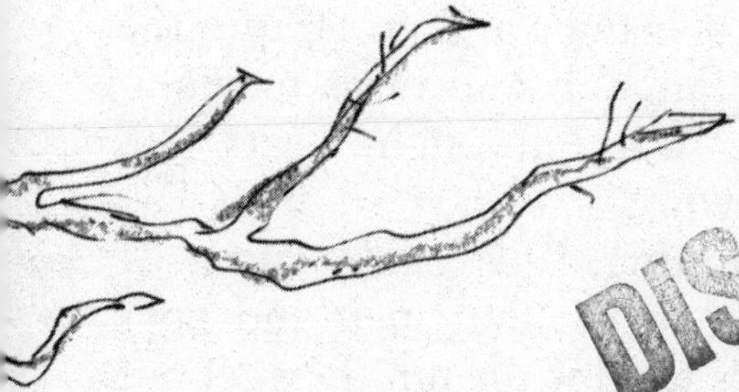

The farm next to ours is owned by Mr and Mrs Gregg. The Greggs have two children, both of them boys. Their names are Philip and William. Sometimes I go over to their farm to play with them.

I am a girl and I am eight years old.

Philip is also eight years old.

William is three years older. He is ten.

What?

Oh, all right, then.

He is eleven.

Last week, something very funny happened to the Gregg family. I am going to tell you about it as best I can.

Now the one thing that Mr Gregg and his two boys loved to do more than anything else was to go hunting. Every Saturday morning they would take their guns and go off into the woods to look for animals and birds to shoot. Even Philip, who was only eight years old, had a gun of his own.

I can't stand hunting. I just can't *stand* it. It doesn't seem right to me that men and boys should kill animals just for the fun they get out of it. So I used to try to stop Philip and William from doing it. Every time I went over to their farm I would do my best to talk them out of it, but they only laughed at me.

I even said something about it once to Mr Gregg, but he just walked on past me as if I wasn't there.

Then, one Saturday morning, I saw Philip and William coming out of the woods with their father, and they were carrying a lovely young deer.

This made me so cross that I started shouting at them.

The boys laughed and made faces at me, and Mr Gregg told me to go home and mind my own P's and Q's.

Well, that did it!

I saw red.

And before I was able to stop myself, I did something I never meant to do.

I PUT THE MAGIC FINGER ON THEM ALL!

Oh, dear! Oh, dear! I even put it on Mrs Gregg, who wasn't there. I put it on the whole Gregg family.

For months I had been telling myself that I would never put the Magic Finger upon anyone again – not after what happened to my teacher, old Mrs Winter.

Poor old Mrs Winter.

One day we were in class, and she was teaching us spelling. 'Stand up,' she said to me, 'and spell cat.'

‘That’s an easy one,’ I said. *‘K-a-t.’*

‘You are a stupid little girl!’ Mrs Winter said.

‘I am not a stupid little girl!’ I cried. ‘I am a very nice little girl!’

‘Go and stand in the corner,’ Mrs Winter said.

Then I got cross, and I saw red, and I put the Magic Finger on Mrs Winter good and strong, and almost at once . . .

Guess what?

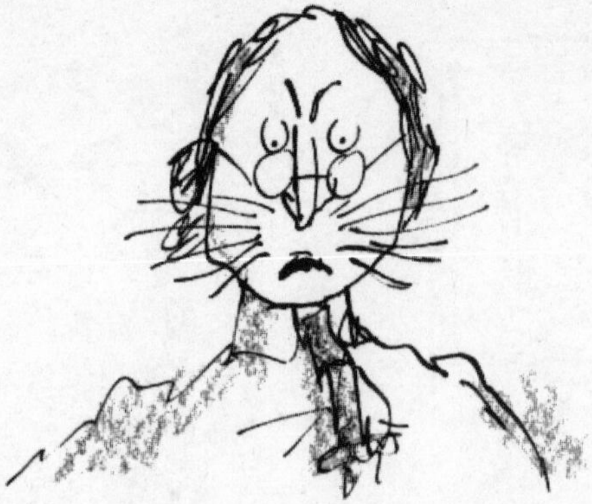

Whiskers began growing out of her face! They were long black whiskers, just like the ones you see on a cat, only much bigger. And how fast they grew! Before we had time to think, they were out to her ears!

Of course the whole class started screaming with laughter, and then Mrs Winter said, 'Will you be so kind as to tell me what you find so madly funny, all of you?'

And when she turned around to write something on the blackboard we saw that she had grown a *tail* as well! It was a huge bushy tail!

I cannot begin to tell you what happened after that, but if any of you are wondering whether Mrs Winter is quite all right again now, the answer is No. And she never will be.

The Magic Finger is something I have been able to do all my life.

I can't tell you just *how* I do it, because I don't even know myself.

But it always happens when I get cross, when I see red . . .

Then I get very, very hot all over . . .

Then the tip of the forefinger of my right hand begins to tingle most terribly . . .

And suddenly a sort of flash comes out of me, a quick flash, like something electric.

It jumps out and touches the person who has made me cross . . .

And after that the Magic Finger is upon him or her, and things begin to happen . . .

Well, the Magic Finger was now upon the whole of the Gregg family, and there was no taking it off again.

I ran home and waited for things to happen.

They happened fast.

I shall now tell you what those things were. I got the whole story from Philip and William the next morning, after it was all over.

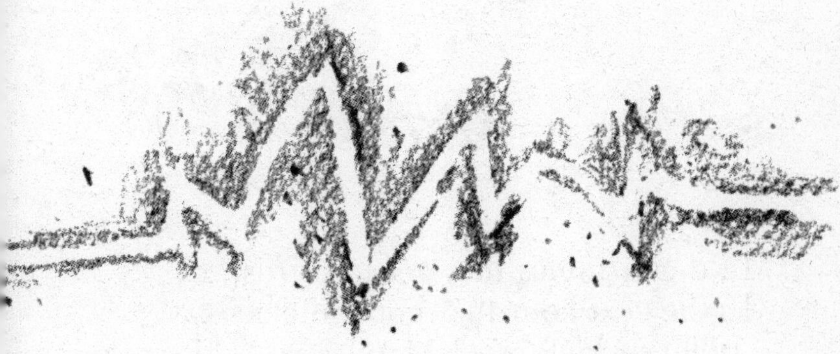

In the afternoon of the very same day that I put the Magic Finger on the Gregg family, Mr Gregg and Philip and William went out hunting once again. This time they were going after wild ducks, so they headed towards the lake.

In the first hour they got ten birds.

In the next hour they got another six.

'What a day!' cried Mr Gregg. 'This is the best yet!' He was beside himself with joy.

Just then four more wild ducks flew over their heads. They were flying very low. They were easy to hit.

BANG! BANG! BANG! BANG! went the guns.

The ducks flew on.

'We missed!' said Mr Gregg. 'That's funny.'

Then, to everyone's surprise, the four ducks turned around and came flying right back to the guns.

'Hey!' said Mr Gregg. 'What on earth are they doing? They are really asking for it this time!' He shot at them again. So did the boys. And again they all missed!

Mr Gregg got very red in the face. ‘It’s the light,’ he said. ‘It’s getting too dark to see. Let’s go home.’

So they started for home, carrying with them the sixteen birds they had shot before.

But the four ducks would not leave them alone. They now began flying around and around the hunters as they walked away.

Mr Gregg did not like it one bit. ‘Be off!’ he cried, and he shot at them many more times, but it was no good. He simply could not hit them. All the way home those four ducks flew around in the sky above their heads, and nothing would make them go away.

Late that night, after Philip and William had gone to bed, Mr Gregg went outside to get some wood for the fire.

He was crossing the yard when all at once he heard the call of a wild duck in the sky.

He stopped and looked up. The night was very still. There was a thin yellow moon over the trees on the hill, and the sky was filled with stars. Then Mr Gregg heard the noise of wings flying low over his head, and he saw the

four ducks, dark against the night sky, flying very close together. They were going around and around the house.

Mr Gregg forgot about the firewood, and hurried back indoors. He was now quite afraid. He did not like what was going on. But he said nothing about it to Mrs Gregg. All he said was, 'Come on, let's go to bed. I feel tired.'

So they went to bed and to sleep.

When morning came, Mr Gregg was the first to wake up.

He opened his eyes.

He was about to put out a hand for his watch, to see the time.

But his hand wouldn't come out.

'That's funny,' he said. 'Where is my hand?'

He lay still, wondering what was up.

Maybe he had hurt that hand in some way?

He tried the other hand.

That wouldn't come out either.

He sat up.

Then, for the first time, he saw what he looked like!

He gave a yell and jumped out of bed.

Mrs Gregg woke up. And when she saw Mr Gregg standing there on the floor, *she* gave a yell, too.

For he was now a tiny little man!

He was maybe as tall as the seat of a chair, but no taller.

And where his arms had been, he had a pair of duck's wings instead!

'But . . . but . . . but . . .' cried Mrs Gregg, going purple in the face. 'My dear man, what's happened to you?'

'What's happened to both of us, you mean!' shouted Mr Gregg.

It was Mrs Gregg's turn now to jump out of bed.

She ran to look at herself in the glass. But she was not tall enough to see into it. She was even smaller than Mr Gregg, and she, too, had got wings instead of arms.

'Oh! Oh! Oh! Oh!' sobbed Mrs Gregg.

'This is witches' work!' cried Mr Gregg. And both of them started running around the room, flapping their wings.

A minute later Philip and William burst in. The same thing had happened to them. They had wings and no arms. And they were *really* tiny. They were about as big as robins.

'Mama! Mama! Mama!' chirruped Philip. 'Look, Mama, we can fly!' And they flew up into the air.

'Come down at once!' said Mrs Gregg. 'You're much too high!' But before she could say another word, Philip and William had flown right out the window.

Mr and Mrs Gregg ran to the window and looked out. The two tiny boys were now high up in the sky.

Then Mrs Gregg said to Mr Gregg, ‘Do you think *we* could do that, my dear?’

‘I don’t see why not,’ Mr Gregg said. ‘Come on, let’s try.’

Mr Gregg began to flap his wings hard, and all at once, up he went.

Then Mrs Gregg did the same.

‘Help!’ she cried as she started going up. ‘Save me!’

‘Come on,’ said Mr Gregg. ‘Don’t be afraid.’

So out the window they flew, far up into the sky, and it did not take them long to catch up with Philip and William.

Soon the whole family was flying around and around together.

'Oh, isn't it lovely!' cried William. 'I've always wanted to know what it feels like to be a bird!'

'Your wings are not getting tired, are they, dear?' Mr Gregg asked Mrs Gregg.

'Not at all,' Mrs Gregg said. 'I could go on for ever!'

'Hey, look down there!' said Philip. 'Somebody is walking in our garden!'

They all looked down, and there below them, in their own garden, they saw four *enormous* wild ducks! The ducks were as big as men, and what is more, they had great long arms, like men, instead of wings.

The ducks were walking in a line to the door of the Greggs' house, swinging their arms and holding their beaks high in the air.

'Stop!' called the tiny Mr Gregg, flying down low over their heads. 'Go away! That's my house!'

The ducks looked up and quacked. The first one put out a hand and opened the door of the house and went in. The others went in after him. The door shut.

The Greggs flew down and sat on the wall near the door. Mrs Gregg began to cry.

'Oh, dear! Oh, dear!' she sobbed. 'They have taken our house. What *shall* we do? We have no place to go!'

Even the boys began to cry a bit now.

'We will be eaten by cats and foxes in the night!' said Philip.

'I want to sleep in my own bed!' said William.

'Now then,' said Mr Gregg. 'It isn't any good crying. That won't help us. Shall I tell you what we are going to do?'

'What?' they said.

Mr Gregg looked at them and smiled. 'We are going to build a nest.'

'A nest!' they said. 'Can we do that?'

'We *must* do it,' said Mr Gregg. 'We've got to have somewhere to sleep. Follow me.'

They flew off to a tall tree, and right at the top of it Mr Gregg chose the place for the nest.

'Now we want sticks,' he said. 'Lots and lots of little sticks. Off you go, all of you, and find them and bring them back here.'

'But we have no hands!' said Philip.

'Then use your mouths.'

Mrs Gregg and the children flew off. Soon they were back, carrying sticks in their mouths.

Mr Gregg took the sticks and started to build the nest.

'More,' he said. 'I want more and more and more sticks. Keep going.'

The nest began to grow. Mr Gregg was very good at making the sticks stick together.

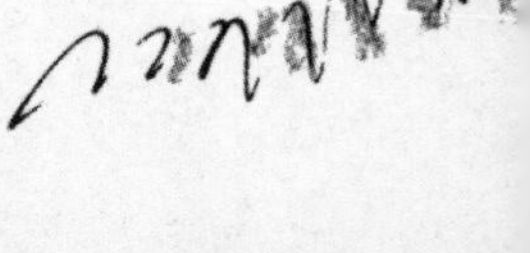

After a while he said, 'That's enough sticks. Now I want leaves and feathers and things like that to make the inside nice and soft.'

The building of the nest went on and on. It took a long time. But at last it was finished.

'Try it,' said Mr Gregg, hopping back. He was very pleased with his work.

'Oh, isn't it lovely!' cried Mrs Gregg, going into it and sitting down. 'I feel I might lay an egg any moment!'

The others all got in beside her.

'How warm it is!' said William.

'And what fun to be living so high up,' said Philip. 'We may be small, but nobody can hurt us up here.'

'But what about food?' said Mrs Gregg. 'We haven't had a thing to eat all day.'

'That's right,' Mr Gregg said. 'So we will now fly back to the house and go in by an open window and get the tin of biscuits when the ducks aren't looking.'

'Oh, we will be pecked to bits by those dirty great ducks!' cried Mrs Gregg.

'We shall be very careful, my love,' said Mr Gregg. And off they went.

But when they got to the house, they found all the windows and doors closed. There was no way in.

'Just look at that beastly duck cooking at my stove!' cried Mrs Gregg as she flew past the kitchen window. 'How dare she!'

'And look at *that* one holding my lovely gun!' shouted Mr Gregg.

'One of them is lying in my bed!' yelled William, looking into a top window.

'And one of them is playing with my electric train!' cried Philip.

'Oh, dear! Oh, dear!' said Mrs Gregg. 'They have taken over our whole house! We shall never get it back. And what *are* we going to eat?'

'I will *not* eat worms,' said Philip. 'I would rather die.'

'Or slugs,' said William.

Mrs Gregg took the two boys under her wings and hugged them. 'Don't worry,' she said. 'I can mince it all up very fine and you won't even know the difference. Lovely slug-burgers. Delicious wormburgers.'

'Oh no!' cried William.

'Never!' said Philip.

'Disgusting!' said Mr Gregg. 'Just because we have wings, we don't have to eat bird food. We shall eat apples instead. Our trees are full of them. Come on!'

So they flew off to an apple tree.

But to eat an apple without holding it in your hands is not at all easy. Every time you try to get your teeth into it, it just pushes away. In the end, they were able to get a few small bites each. And then it began to get dark, so they all flew back to the nest and lay down to sleep.

It must have been at about this time that I, back in my own house, picked up the telephone and tried to call Philip. I wanted to see if the family was all right.

'Hello,' I said.

'Quack!' said a voice at the other end.

'Who is it?' I asked.

'Quack-quack!'

'Philip,' I said, 'is that you?'

'Quack-quack-quack-quack-quack!'

'Oh, stop it!' I said.

Then there came a very funny noise. It was like a bird laughing.

I put down the telephone quickly.

'Oh, that Magic Finger!' I cried. 'What *has* it done to my friends?'

That night, while Mr and Mrs Gregg and Philip and William were trying to get some sleep up in the high nest, a great wind began to blow. The tree rocked from side to side, and everyone, even Mr Gregg, was afraid that the

nest would fall down. Then came the rain. It rained and rained, and the water ran into the nest and they all got as wet as could be – and oh, it was a bad, bad night!

At last the morning came, and with it the warm sun.

'Well!' said Mrs Gregg. 'Thank goodness that's over! I never want to sleep in a nest again!' She got up and looked over the side . . .

'Help!' she cried. 'Look! Look down there!'

'What is it, my love?' said Mr Gregg. He stood up and peeped over the side.

He got the surprise of his life!

On the ground below them stood the four enormous ducks, as tall as men, and three of them were holding guns in their hands. One had Mr Gregg's gun, one had Philip's gun, and one had William's gun.

The guns were all pointing right up at the nest.

'No! No! No!' called out Mr and Mrs Gregg, both together. 'Don't shoot! Please don't shoot!'

'Why not?' said one of the ducks. It was the one who wasn't holding a gun. 'You are always shooting at *us*.'

'Oh, but that's not the same!' said Mr Gregg. 'We are *allowed* to shoot ducks!'

'Who allows you?' asked the duck.

'We allow each other,' said Mr Gregg.

'Very nice,' said the duck. 'And now *we* are going to allow each other to shoot you.'

(I would have loved to have seen Mr Gregg's face just then.)

'Oh, *please*!' cried Mrs Gregg. 'My two little children are up here with us! You wouldn't shoot my *children*!'

'Yesterday you shot *my* children,' said the duck. 'You shot all six of my children.'

'I'll never do it again!' cried Mr Gregg. 'Never, never, never!'

'Do you really mean that?' asked the duck.

'I *do* mean it!' said Mr Gregg. 'I'll never shoot another duck as long as I live!'

'That is not good enough,' said the duck. 'What about deer?'

'I'll do anything you say if you will only put down those guns!' cried Mr Gregg. 'I'll never shoot another duck or another deer or anything else again!'

'Will you give me your word on that?' said the duck.

'I will! I will!' said Mr Gregg.

'Will you throw away your guns?' asked the duck.

'I will break them into tiny bits!' said Mr Gregg. 'And never again need you be afraid of me or my family.'

'Very well,' said the duck. 'You may now come down. And by the way, may I congratulate you on the nest. For a first effort it's pretty good.'

Mr and Mrs Gregg and Philip and William hopped out of the nest and flew down.

Then all at once everything went black before their eyes, and they couldn't see. At the

same time a funny feeling came over them all, and they heard a great wind blowing in their ears.

Then the black that was before their eyes turned to blue, to green, to red, and then to gold, and suddenly, there they were, standing

in lovely bright sunshine in their own garden, near their own house, and everything was back to normal once again.

'Our wings have gone!' cried Mr Gregg. 'And our arms have come back!'

'And we are not tiny any more!' laughed Mrs Gregg. 'Oh, I am so glad!'

Philip and William began dancing about with joy.

Then, high above their heads, they heard the call of a wild duck. They all looked up, and they saw the four birds, lovely against the blue sky, flying very close together, heading back to the lake in the woods.

It must have been about half an hour later that I myself walked into the Greggs' garden. I had come to see how things were going, and I must admit I was expecting the worst. At the gate I stopped and stared. It was a queer sight.

In one corner Mr Gregg was smashing all three guns into tiny pieces with a huge hammer.

In another corner Mrs Gregg was placing beautiful flowers upon sixteen tiny mounds of soil which I learned later were the graves of the ducks that had been shot the day before.

And in the middle of the yard stood Philip and William, with a sack of their father's best barley beside them. They were surrounded by ducks, doves, pigeons, sparrows, robins, larks, and many other kinds that I did not know, and the birds were eating the barley that the boys were scattering by the handful.

'Good morning, Mr Gregg,' I said.

Mr Gregg lowered his hammer and looked at me. 'My name is not Gregg any more,' he said. 'In honour of my feathered friends, I have changed it from Gregg to Egg.'

'And I am Mrs Egg,' said Mrs Gregg.

'What happened?' I asked. They seemed to have gone completely dotty, all four of them.

Philip and William then began to tell me the whole story. When they had finished, William said, 'Look! There's the nest! Can you see it? Right up in the top of the tree! That's where we slept last night!'

'I built it *all* myself,' Mr Egg said proudly. 'Every stick of it.'

'If you don't believe us,' Mrs Egg said, 'just go into the house and take a look at the bathroom. It's a mess.'

'They filled the tub right up to the brim,' Philip said. 'They must have been swimming around in it all night! And feathers everywhere!'

'Ducks like water,' Mr Egg said. 'I'm glad they had a good time.'

Just then, from somewhere over by the lake, there came a loud BANG!

'Someone's shooting!' I cried.

'That'll be Jim Cooper,' Mr Egg said. 'Him and his three boys. They're shooting mad, those Coopers are, the whole family.'

Suddenly I started to see red . . .

Then I got very hot all over . . .

Then the tip of my finger began tingling most terribly. I could feel the power building up and up inside me . . .

I turned and started running towards the lake as fast as I could.

'Hey!' shouted Mr Egg. 'What's up? Where are you going?'

'To find the Coopers,' I called back.

'But why?'

'You wait and see!' I said. 'They'll be nesting in the trees tonight, every one of them!'

TURN THE PAGE FOR A LOOK AT ANOTHER SCRUMDIDDLYUMPTIOUS STORY FROM ROALD DAHL!

The Reader of Books

It's a funny thing about mothers and fathers. Even when their own child is the most disgusting little blister you could ever imagine, they still think that he or she is wonderful.

Some parents go further. They become so blinded by adoration they manage to convince themselves their child has qualities of genius.

Well, there is nothing very wrong with all this. It's the way of the world. It is only when the parents begin telling *us* about the brilliance of their own revolting offspring, that we start shouting, "Bring us a basin! We're going to be sick!"

School teachers suffer a good deal from having to listen to this sort of twaddle from proud parents, but they usually get their own back when the time comes to write the end-of-term reports. If I were a teacher I would cook up some real scorchers for the children of doting parents. "Your son Maximilian", I would write, "is a total wash-out. I hope you have a family business you can push him into when he leaves school because he sure as heck won't get a job anywhere else." Or if I were feeling lyrical that day, I might write, "It is a curious truth that grasshoppers have their hearing-organs in the sides of the abdomen. Your daughter Vanessa, judging by what she's learnt this term, has no hearing-organs at all."

I might even delve deeper into natural history and say, "The periodical cicada spends six years as a grub underground, and no more than six *days* as a free creature of sunlight and air. Your son Wilfred has spent six years as a grub in this school and we are still waiting for him to emerge from the chrysalis." A particularly poisonous little girl might sting me into saying, "Fiona has the same glacial beauty as an iceberg, but unlike the iceberg she has absolutely nothing below the surface." I

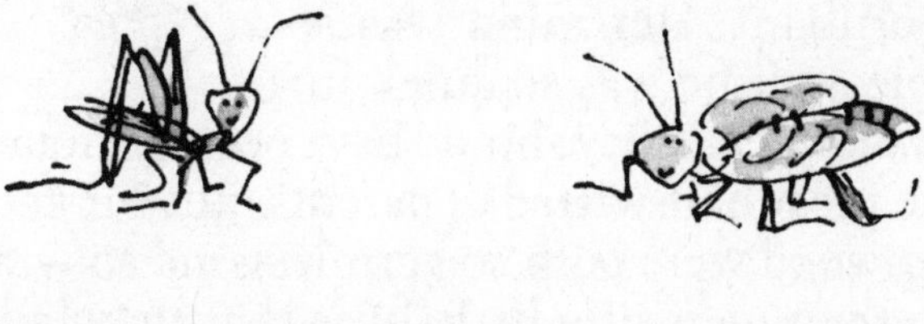

think I might enjoy writing end-of-term reports for the stinkers in my class. But enough of that. We have to get on.

Occasionally one comes across parents who take the opposite line, who show no interest at all in their children, and these of course are far worse than the doting ones. Mr and Mrs Wormwood were two such parents. They had a son called Michael and a daughter called Matilda, and the parents looked upon Matilda in particular as nothing more than a scab. A scab is something you have to put up with until the time comes when you can pick it off and flick it away. Mr and Mrs Wormwood looked forward enormously to the time when they could pick their little daughter off and flick her away, preferably into the next county or even further than that.

It is bad enough when parents treat *ordinary* children as though they were scabs and bunions, but it becomes somehow a lot worse when the child in question is *extraordinary*, and by that I mean sensitive and brilliant. Matilda was both of these things, but above all she was brilliant. Her mind was so nimble and she was so quick to learn that her ability should have been obvious even to the most half-witted of parents. But Mr and Mrs Wormwood were both so gormless and so wrapped up in their own silly little lives that they failed to notice anything unusual about their daughter. To tell the truth, I doubt they would have noticed had she crawled into the house with a broken leg.

Matilda's brother Michael was a perfectly normal boy, but the sister, as I said, was something to make your eyes pop. By the age of *one and a half* her speech was perfect and she knew as many words as most grown-ups. The parents, instead of applauding her, called her a noisy chatterbox and told her sharply that small girls should be seen and not heard.

By the time she was *three*, Matilda had taught herself to read by studying newspapers and magazines that lay around the house. At the age of *four*, she could read fast and well and she naturally began hankering after books. The only book in the whole of this enlightened household was something called *Easy Cooking* belonging to her mother, and when she had read this from cover to cover and had learnt all the recipes by heart, she decided she wanted something more interesting.

"Daddy," she said, "do you think you could buy me a book?"

"A *book*?" he said. "What d'you want a flaming book for?"

"To read, Daddy."

"What's wrong with the telly, for heaven's sake? We've got a lovely telly with a twelve-inch screen and now you come asking for a book! You're getting spoiled, my girl!"

Nearly every weekday afternoon Matilda was left alone in the house. Her brother (five years older than her) went to school. Her father went to work and her mother went out playing bingo in a town eight miles away. Mrs Wormwood was hooked on bingo and played it five afternoons a week. On the afternoon of the day when her father had refused to buy her a book, Matilda set out all by herself to walk to the public library in the village. When she arrived, she introduced herself to the librarian, Mrs Phelps. She asked if she might sit awhile and read a book. Mrs Phelps, slightly taken aback at the arrival of such a tiny girl unacccompanied by a parent, nevertheless told her she was very welcome.

"Where are the children's books please?" Matilda asked.

"They're over there on those lower shelves," Mrs Phelps told her. "Would you like me to help you find a nice one with lots of pictures in it?"

"No, thank you," Matilda said. "I'm sure I can manage."

From then on, every afternoon, as soon as her mother had left for bingo, Matilda would toddle down to the library. The walk took only ten minutes and this allowed her two glorious hours sitting quietly by herself in a cosy corner devouring one book after another. When she had read every single children's book in the place, she started wandering round in search of something else.

Mrs Phelps, who had been watching her with fascination for the past few weeks, now got up from her desk and went over to her. "Can I help you, Matilda?" she asked.

"I'm wondering what to read next," Matilda said. "I've finished all the children's books."

"You mean you've looked at the pictures?"

"Yes, but I've read the books as well."

Mrs Phelps looked down at Matilda from her great height and Matilda looked right back up at her.

"I thought some were very poor," Matilda said, "but others were lovely. I liked *The Secret Garden* best of all. It was full of mystery. The mystery of

the room behind the closed door and the mystery of the garden behind the big wall."

Mrs Phelps was stunned. "Exactly how old are you, Matilda?" she asked.

"Four years and three months," Matilda said.

Mrs Phelps was more stunned than ever, but she had the sense not to show it. "What sort of a book would you like to read next?" she asked.

Matilda said, "I would like a really good one that grown-ups read. A famous one. I don't know any names."

Mrs Phelps looked along the shelves, taking her time. She didn't quite know what to bring out. How, she asked herself, does one choose a famous grown-up book for a four-year-old girl? Her first thought was to pick a young teenager's romance of the kind that is written for fifteen-year-old school-girls, but for some reason she found herself instinctively walking past that particular shelf.

"Try this," she said at last. "It's very famous and very good. If it's too long for you, just let me know and I'll find something shorter and a bit easier."

"*Great Expectations,*" Matilda read, "by Charles Dickens. I'd love to try it."

I must be mad, Mrs Phelps told herself, but to Matilda she said, "Of course you may try it."

Over the next few afternoons Mrs Phelps could hardly take her eyes from the small girl sitting for hour after hour in the big armchair at the far end of the room with the book on her lap. It was necessary to rest it on the lap because it was too heavy for her to hold up, which meant she had to sit leaning forward in order to read. And a strange sight it was, this tiny dark-haired person sitting there with her feet nowhere near touching the floor, totally absorbed in the wonderful adventures of Pip and old Miss Havisham and her cobwebbed house and by the spell of magic that Dickens the great story-teller had woven with his words. The only movement from the reader was the lifting of the hand every now and then to turn over a page, and Mrs Phelps always felt sad when the time came for her to cross the floor and say, "It's ten to five, Matilda."

During the first week of Matilda's visits Mrs Phelps had said to her, "Does your mother walk you down here every day and then take you home?"

"My mother goes to Aylesbury every afternoon to play bingo," Matilda had said. "She doesn't know I come here."

"But that's surely not right," Mrs Phelps said. "I think you'd better ask her."

"I'd rather not," Matilda said. "She doesn't encourage reading books. Nor does my father."

"But what do they expect you to do every afternoon in an empty house?"

"Just mooch around and watch the telly."

"I see."

"She doesn't really care what I do," Matilda said a little sadly.

Mrs Phelps was concerned about the child's safety on the walk through the fairly busy village High Street and the crossing of the road, but she decided not to interfere.

Within a week, Matilda had finished *Great Expectations* which in that edition contained four hundred and eleven pages. "I loved it," she said to Mrs Phelps. "Has Mr Dickens written any others?"

"A great number," said the astounded Mrs Phelps. "Shall I choose you another?"

Over the next six months, under Mrs Phelps's

watchful and compassionate eye, Matilda read the following books:

Nicholas Nickleby by Charles Dickens
Oliver Twist by Charles Dickens
Jane Eyre by Charlotte Brontë
Pride and Prejudice by Jane Austen
Tess of the D'Urbervilles by Thomas Hardy
Gone to Earth by Mary Webb
Kim by Rudyard Kipling
The Invisible Man by H. G. Wells
The Old Man and the Sea by Ernest Hemingway
The Sound and the Fury by William Faulkner
The Grapes of Wrath by John Steinbeck
The Good Companions by J. B. Priestley
Brighton Rock by Graham Greene
Animal Farm by George Orwell

It was a formidable list and by now Mrs Phelps was filled with wonder and excitement, but it was probably a good thing that she did not allow herself to be completely carried away by it all. Almost anyone else witnessing the achievements of this small child would have been tempted to make a great fuss and shout the news all over the village and beyond, but not so Mrs Phelps. She was someone who minded her own business and had long since discovered it was seldom worth while to interfere with other people's children.

"Mr Hemingway says a lot of things I don't understand," Matilda said to her. "Especially about men and women. But I loved it all the same. The way he tells it I feel I am right there on the spot watching it all happen."

"A fine writer will always make you feel that," Mrs Phelps said. "And don't worry about the bits you can't understand. Sit back and allow the words to wash around you, like music."

"I will, I will."

"Did you know", Mrs Phelps said, "that public libraries like this allow you to borrow books and take them home?"

"I didn't know that," Matilda said. "Could *I* do it?"

"Of course," Mrs Phelps said. "When you have chosen the book you want, bring it to me so I can make a note of it and it's yours for two weeks. You can take more than one if you wish."

From then on, Matilda would visit the library only once a week in order to take out new books and return the old ones. Her own small bedroom now became her reading-room and there she would sit and read most afternoons, often with a mug of hot chocolate beside her. She was not quite tall enough to reach things around the kitchen, but she kept a small box in the outhouse which she brought in and stood on in order to get whatever she wanted. Mostly it was hot chocolate she made, warming the milk in a saucepan on the stove before mixing it. Occasionally she made Bovril or Ovaltine. It was pleasant to take a hot drink up to her room and have it beside her as she sat in her silent room reading in the empty house in the afternoons. The books transported her into new worlds and introduced her to amazing people who lived exciting lives. She went on olden-day sailing ships with Joseph Conrad. She went to Africa with Ernest Hemingway and to India with Rudyard Kipling. She travelled all over the world while sitting in her little room in an English village.

READ MORE FROM ROALD DAHL, THE WORLD'S NO.1 STORYTELLER!

1
Here Comes Charlie

THESE TWO VERY OLD PEOPLE are the father and mother of Mr. Bucket. Their names are Grandpa Joe and Grandma Josephine.

And *these* two very old people are the father and mother of Mrs. Bucket. Their names are Grandpa George and Grandma Georgina.

This is Mr. Bucket. This is Mrs. Bucket.

Mr. and Mrs. Bucket have a small boy whose name is Charlie Bucket.

This is Charlie.

How d'you do? And how d'you do? And how d'you do again?

He is pleased to meet you.

The whole of this family—the six grownups (count them) and little Charlie Bucket—live together in a small wooden house on the edge of a great town.

The house wasn't nearly large enough for so many people, and life was extremely uncomfortable for them all. There were only two rooms in the place altogether, and there was only one bed. The bed was given to the four old grandparents because they were so old and tired. They were so tired, they never got out of it.

Grandpa Joe and Grandma Josephine on this side, Grandpa George and Grandma Georgina on this side.

Mr. and Mrs. Bucket and little Charlie Bucket slept in the other room, upon mattresses on the floor.

In the summertime, this wasn't too bad, but in the winter, freezing cold drafts blew across the floor all night long, and it was awful.

There wasn't any question of them being able to buy a better house—or even one more bed to sleep in. They were far too poor for that.

Mr. Bucket was the only person in the family with a job. He worked in a toothpaste factory, where he sat all day long at a bench and screwed the little caps onto the tops of the tubes of toothpaste after the tubes had been filled. But a toothpaste cap-screwer is never paid very much money, and poor Mr. Bucket, however hard he worked, and however fast he screwed on the caps, was never able to make enough to buy one-half of the things that so large a family needed. There wasn't even enough money to buy proper food for them all. The only meals they could afford were bread and margarine for breakfast, boiled potatoes and cabbage for lunch, and cabbage soup for supper. Sundays were a bit better. They all looked forward to Sundays because then, although they had exactly the same, everyone was allowed a second helping.

The Buckets, of course, didn't starve, but every one of them—the two old grandfathers, the two old grandmothers, Charlie's father, Charlie's mother, and especially little Charlie himself—went about from morning till night with a horrible empty feeling in their tummies.

Charlie felt it worst of all. And although his father and

mother often went without their own share of lunch or supper so that they could give it to him, it still wasn't nearly enough for a growing boy. He desperately wanted something more filling and satisfying than cabbage and cabbage soup. The one thing he longed for more than anything else was . . . CHOCOLATE.

Walking to school in the mornings, Charlie could see great slabs of chocolate piled up high in the shop windows, and he would stop and stare and press his nose against the glass, his mouth watering like mad. Many times a day, he would see other children taking creamy candy bars out of their pockets and munching them greedily, and *that*, of course, was *pure* torture.

Only once a year, on his birthday, did Charlie Bucket ever get to taste a bit of chocolate. The whole family saved up their money for that special occasion, and when the great day arrived, Charlie was always presented with one small chocolate bar to eat all by himself. And each time he received it, on those marvelous birthday mornings, he would place it carefully in a small wooden box that he owned, and treasure it as though it were a bar of solid gold; and for the next few days, he would allow himself only to look at it, but never to touch it. Then at last, when he could stand it no longer, he would peel back a *tiny* bit of the paper wrapping at one corner to expose a *tiny* bit of chocolate, and then he would take a *tiny* nibble—just enough to allow the lovely sweet taste to spread out slowly over his tongue. The next day, he would take another tiny nibble, and so on, and so on. And in this way, Charlie would make his ten-cent bar of birthday chocolate last him for more than a month.

But I haven't yet told you about the one awful thing that tortured little Charlie, the lover of chocolate, more than *anything* else. This thing, for him, was far, far worse than seeing slabs of chocolate in the shop windows or watching other children munching creamy candy bars right in front of him. It was the most terrible torturing thing you could imagine, and it was this:

In the town itself, actually within *sight* of the house in which Charlie lived, there was an ENORMOUS CHOCOLATE FACTORY!

Just imagine that!

And it wasn't simply an ordinary enormous chocolate factory, either. It was the largest and most famous in the whole world! It was WONKA'S FACTORY, owned by a man called Mr. Willy Wonka, the greatest inventor and maker of chocolates that there has ever been. And what a tremendous, marvelous place it was! It had huge iron gates leading in to it, and a high wall surrounding it, and smoke belching from its chimneys, and strange whizzing sounds coming from deep inside it. And outside the walls, for half a mile around in every direction, the air was scented with the heavy rich smell of melting chocolate!

Twice a day, on his way to and from school, little Charlie Bucket had to walk right past the gates of the factory. And every time he went by, he would begin to walk very, very slowly, and he would hold his nose high in the air and take long deep sniffs of the gorgeous chocolatey smell all around him.

Oh, how he loved that smell!

And oh, how he wished he could go inside the factory and see what it was like!

2
Mr. Willy Wonka's Factory

In the evenings, after he had finished his supper of watery cabbage soup, Charlie always went into the room of his four grandparents to listen to their stories, and then afterwards to say good night.

Every one of these old people was over ninety. They were as shriveled as prunes, and as bony as skeletons, and throughout the day, until Charlie made his appearance, they lay huddled in their one bed, two at either end, with nightcaps on to keep their heads warm, dozing the time away with nothing to do. But as soon as they heard the door opening, and heard Charlie's voice saying, "Good evening, Grandpa Joe and Grandma Josephine, and Grandpa George and Grandma Georgina," then all four of them would suddenly sit up, and their old wrinkled faces would light up with smiles of pleasure—and the talking would begin. For they loved this little boy. He was the only bright thing in their lives, and his evening visits were something that they looked forward to all day long. Often, Charlie's mother and father would come in as well, and stand by the door, listening to the stories that the old people told; and thus, for perhaps half an hour every night, this room would become a happy place, and the whole family would forget that it was hungry and poor.

One evening, when Charlie went in to see his grandparents, he said to them, "Is it *really* true that Wonka's

Chocolate Factory is the biggest in the world?"

"True?" cried all four of them at once. "Of course it's true! Good heavens, didn't you know *that*? It's about *fifty* times as big as any other!"

"And is Mr. Willy Wonka *really* the cleverest chocolate maker in the world?"

"My *dear* boy," said Grandpa Joe, raising himself up a little higher on his pillow, "Mr. Willy Wonka is the most *amazing,* the most *fantastic,* the most *extraordinary* chocolate maker the world has ever seen! I thought *everybody* knew that!"

"I knew he was famous, Grandpa Joe, and I knew he was very clever. . . ."

"Clever!" cried the old man. "He's more than that! He's a *magician* with chocolate! He can make *anything*—anything he wants! Isn't that a fact, my dears?"

The other three old people nodded their heads slowly up and down, and said, "*Absolutely* true. *Just* as true as can be."

And Grandpa Joe said, "You mean to say I've never *told* you about Mr. Willy Wonka and his factory?"

"Never," answered little Charlie.

"Good heavens above! I don't know what's the matter with me!"

"Will you tell me now, Grandpa Joe, please?"

"I certainly will. Sit down beside me on the bed, my dear, and listen carefully."

Grandpa Joe was the oldest of the four grandparents. He was ninety-six and a half, and that is just about as old as anybody can be. Like all extremely old people, he was delicate and weak, and throughout the day he spoke very little. But in the evenings, when Charlie, his beloved grandson, was in the room, he seemed in some marvelous way to grow quite young again. All his tiredness fell away from him, and he became as eager and excited as a young boy.

"Oh, what a man he is, this Mr. Willy Wonka!" cried Grandpa Joe. "Did you know, for example, that he has himself invented more than two hundred new kinds of candy bars, each with a different center, each far sweeter and creamier and more delicious than anything the other chocolate factories can make!"

"Perfectly true!" cried Grandma Josephine. "And he sends them to *all* the four corners of the earth! Isn't that so, Grandpa Joe?"

"It is, my dear, it is. And to all the kings and presidents of the world as well. But it isn't only candy bars that he makes. Oh, dear me, no! He has some really *fantastic* inventions up his sleeve, Mr. Willy Wonka has! Did you know that he's invented a way of making chocolate ice cream so that it stays cold for hours and hours without being in the icebox?

You can even leave it lying in the sun all morning on a hot day and it won't go runny!"

"But that's *impossible*!" said little Charlie, staring at his grandfather.

"Of course it's impossible!" cried Grandpa Joe. "It's completely *absurd*! But Mr. Willy Wonka has done it!"

"Quite right!" the others agreed, nodding their heads. "Mr. Wonka has done it."

"And then again," Grandpa Joe went on, speaking very slowly now so that Charlie wouldn't miss a word, "Mr. Willy Wonka can make marshmallows that taste of violets, and rich caramels that change color every ten seconds as you suck them, and little feathery sweets that melt away deliciously the moment you put them between your lips. He can make chewing gum that never loses its taste, and candy balloons that you can blow up to enormous sizes before you pop them with a pin and gobble them up. And, by a most secret method, he can make lovely blue birds' eggs with black spots on them, and when you put one of these in your mouth, it gradually gets smaller

and smaller until suddenly there is nothing left except a tiny little pink sugary baby bird sitting on the tip of your tongue."

Grandpa Joe paused and ran the point of his tongue slowly over his lips. "It makes my mouth water just *thinking* about it," he said.

"Mine, too," said little Charlie. "But *please* go on."

STORIES ARE GOOD FOR **YOU.**

Roald Dahl said,
"If you have good thoughts, they will shine out of your face like sunbeams and you will always look lovely."

We believe in doing good things.
That's why 10 percent of all Roald Dahl income* goes to our charity partners. We have supported causes including: specialist children's nurses, grants for families in need, and educational outreach programs. Thank you for helping us to sustain this vital work.

Find out more at roalddahl.com

* All author payments and royalty income net of third-party commissions.